D0375063

ISLANDS OF ICE
The Story of a Harp Seal

To Alexandra, Kyle and Kelsie, who bring me infinite joy—K.M.H.

To my family for their support and Nonno Paolo for his inspiration—J.P.G.

Published by Soundprints Division of Trudy Corporation, Norwalk, Connecticut.

Book layout: Marcin D. Pilchowski
Editor: Judy Gitenstein
Editorial assistance: Chelsea Shriver

First Edition 2001
10 9 8 7 6 5 4 3 2
Printed in China

Acknowledgments:
  Our very special thanks to Dr. Don E. Wilson of the Department of Vertebrate Zoology at the Smithsonian Institution's National Museum of Natural History for his curatorial review.

Soundprints
Where Children Discover...

by Kathleen M. Hollenbeck   Illustrated by John Paul Genzo

ISLANDS OF ICE
The Story of a Harp Seal

An icy wind howls off the eastern coast of Canada. It races over dark, frigid water in the Gulf of St. Lawrence and across ice floes, great islands of ice on the sea. It is early March. Just before sunrise, a harp seal lies on the snowy ice. She groans and twists her body. As the blackness of night retreats to a thin veil of gray, she gives birth to a tiny harp seal. Seal Pup lies on the snow, fur wet and tinted yellow. Her thin body shivers in the cold.

The mother seal licks her pup's fur and inhales its distinctive scent. Seal Pup cries, and her mother listens carefully. Then she rolls on her side, and the pup drinks her rich, creamy milk. At twenty pounds, the pup looks small beside her mother, who weighs nearly 300 pounds. The pup will nurse about five times a day for two weeks. She will gain weight quickly, growing a thick layer of blubber to protect her from the cold.

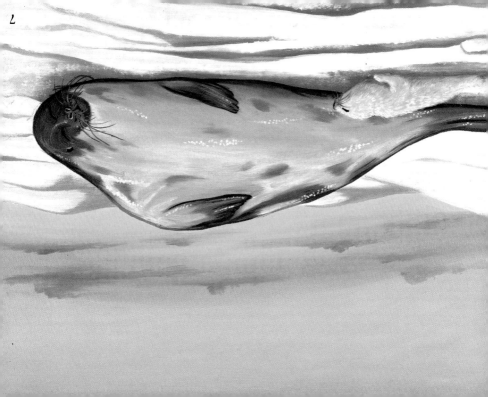

Seal Pup and her mother are not alone. The ice floe, which stretches for miles, is a floating nursery for thousands of seal pups. As gulls wail and winds howl, Seal Pup falls asleep. Digging sharp claws into the ice, her mother pulls herself to a bobbing hole. She used her claws to carve this hole in the ice before her pup was born. Now she slides through the bobbing hole into the water. There with a herd of adult seals, she swims and catches fish. She pops her head through the hole now and then and peeks at her pup.

Two days pass. Seal Pup's coat is now white. Sun shines through her fur, warming the dark skin below. Again, the mother seal has swum off to hunt for food. This time, Seal Pup wakes while her mother is gone. She is hungry and cold. Her cries ring out over the ice. Her newborn eyes see only shadows. She spies a dark shape and drags herself toward it.

It is a mother seal, but she will feed only her own. She waves her front flippers and makes a shrill noise, warning the unfamiliar seal pup to stay away.

Seal Pup is hungry and must have food. She moves closer. The mother snarls and smacks Seal Pup with her flippers, knocking her back. Crawling this way and that, she searches for her mother. Finally, she huddles on the ice and cries.

Just then, the mother seal pulls herself from the water and sniffs the air for her pup's scent. She hears her pup's cry and crawls toward it. She sniffs to be sure the seal is hers. Seal Pup crawls near, but her mother moves backward and slowly leads her to nurse at the bobbing hole.

That night, a storm rises. The ice floe rocks violently on the water and begins to break apart. Seals slide into the dark, icy sea. Young pups drown for they cannot swim. Seal Pup clings to the ice with her claws. So does her mother. They hear seals cry as floes crash together and break apart. Side-by-side, they wait for the storm to end.

Seal Pup is two weeks old. Her mother swims as usual. But this time, she does not return. Like all harp seal mothers, she stays with the adult herd, leaving her pup forever. Now Seal Pup must learn to survive on her own.

For days, the pup lies on the ice, crying. She does not eat or drink. Her body gets nutrients from the fat she has stored since birth. All around her, pups cry. At last, they crawl to one another. Seal Pup's new life with a herd has begun.

About this time, Seal Pup begins to molt. She sheds her white fur for a new coat of rough gray hair. Molting takes several days, and it itches. Seal Pup rubs against the ice to ease the itch. White fur clings to her in patches.

Within days, Seal Pup's coat is completely gray. She crawls to the edge of the ice, joining other pups there. They stand together, peering down at the water.

19

Though born right beside it, Seal Pup has never seen water. She leans forward to sniff and falls in with a splash, feeling the water's cold grip for the very first time. Seal Pup tries to get out and claws at the ice. Instinctively, she dives underwater. Her flippers move back and forth. They seem to beat against the sea. In seconds, others join her. They swim and dive about.

Seal Pup spends most of her time in the water. She catches shrimp-like animals and small fish. She splashes and dives. She can stay underwater for up to thirty minutes. Underwater, her nose is tightly shut. It opens when she comes up for air.

Seal Pup sleeps in the water, her nose just below the surface and her body hanging down. Every five minutes, her back flippers flap, pushing her body up and her nose out of the water. She breathes deeply and sinks under again, still asleep.

For most of her life, Seal Pup has known little danger. Then one morning, sharks weave among the seals. Seal Pup swims under a patch of ice to dig an escape hole. The ice is too thick, though, and she cannot scratch through it. Seal Pup claws faster. She is running out of air. At last she finds a thin spot and digs a hole for her nose. She breathes, makes the hole larger, and pulls herself out of the water. Safe at last, she stretches out on the ice.

25

Before long, it's June, and the Gulf waters grow warmer. The adult herd heads north to cooler waters separated from the pups.

The pups head north too, far behind the adults. They travel alone or in small groups, resting and feeding by day. Each night, they swim ten to twenty miles, traveling 2,000 miles in all. The trip will take almost three months. By instinct, they know where to go.

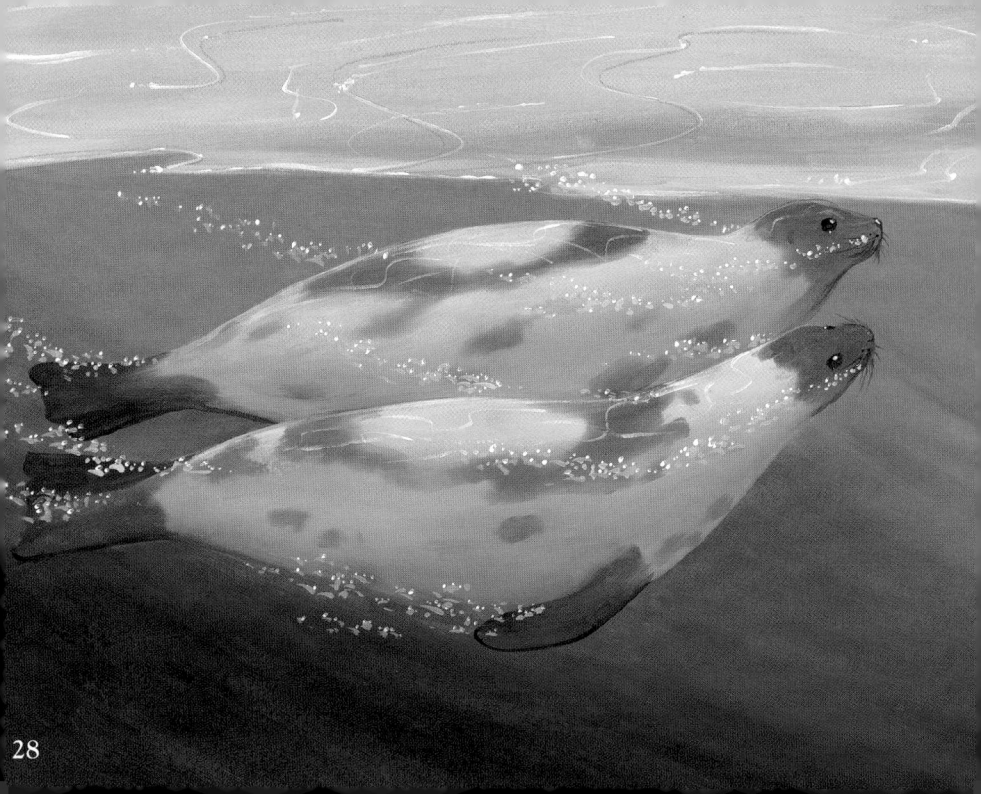

Months pass, and winter approaches. The harp seals return to the Gulf of St. Lawrence. This time, Seal Pup swims with the adult herd. She is one year old now and nearly as large as her mother. She eats big fish such as capelin, polar cod, and herring.

Back in the Gulf one morning, Seal Pup peeks out of the water at the edge of an ice floe. She watches young seals on the ice, crying for food and the warmth of their mothers. It will be several years before she will climb onto the ice and give birth to her own pup. Until then, she will travel with the herd.

Each spring for the rest of her life, she will swim north to the waters of the North Atlantic Ocean. Each fall, she will go south to the Gulf of St. Lawrence. She will find what she needs in cold waters, always at home among islands of ice.

About Harp Seals

Harp seals are named for the black, harp-shaped pattern that adorns the back and shoulders of the adults. The largest population of harp seals lives in the Baffin Bay area of the Labrador Sea and the Gulf of St. Lawrence, migrating between the two each spring and fall. Smaller herds live in the White Sea and the Greenland Sea, north of Iceland.

In late February and early March, thousands of mature female seals stretch out on thick ice floes in the Gulf of St. Lawrence. Male seals in the herd swim nearby while the females give birth and nurse. Two weeks after their pups are born, the females rejoin the males, forgetting the scent and sound of their own pups forever. The pups form a herd of their own, living apart from adults until they are at least one year old.

Harp seals are pinnipeds, animals that have flippers in place of hands and feet. Their hind flippers stick straight out from their bodies and provide power and speed in the water. The front flippers, like hands and arms, are found on both sides of the body. These help pull the seals across the ice and help them steer in the water.

Harp seals depend on instinct and senses to navigate during migration. Whiskers on their noses sense water temperature, the location and movement of ice floes and the presence of food and animals. Their eyes spot darting fish and predators, helping them find food and avoid danger. Their ears pick up sound waves underwater, helping them stay on course.

Glossary

bobbing hole: A round opening carved in an ice floe by an adult seal and used to enter and exit the sea.
ice floe: A sheet of floating ice.